Saving Wor....

A Central Pennsylvania Novel

of History and Mystery

Paul C. Nelson

For my dad, Russ Nelson

(1931-2016)

Thank you Lindsay Kalbach, Kathy McClintic, and Colleen McGowan Hardin, for reading, and helping with revisions.

Thank you Will Hiles for touching up the cover photo, and for inspiration. Will is a great writer, artist, and an even better friend. He's also an adequate fisherman.

Chapter 1

Jess McKivison stood in her yard in the little town of Renfro, Pennsylvania. By all accounts, it was a perfect autumn day. Jess's little boy, Abe, was playing by her side. The sun was bright, and still warm for October. The Susquehanna River flowed swiftly by the edge of the property. Normally, the sound of the water calmed Jess. She would often sit in her yard for hours listening to it. Today, however, it drove her nearly insane. She was in a complete panic. Her teenage daughter, Emily, had not come home after school. It was now almost six-o-clock. Emily was always home by three-thirty. Jess had called all over town, but nobody had seen Emily since just after school. Jess put her head down and held her hands over her ears.

She screamed, "Emily no!!! NOT MY EMILY!"

Abe looked at her and gave out a concerned whimper. There had to be an explanation. Emily would never run off with anyone. She was a model student, completely honest and trustworthy. She was a reliable babysitter for several families, and always helped Jess with Abe. She was the leader in her church youth group and helped in the nursery during Sunday school. She was a good kid! Something had to have happened.

Jess took out her phone once again. This time she called her friend-police chief Warren Dale. Warren would know what to do. Every nerve, every muscle in Jess's body was taught. The sound of the river roared in her ears. Yet, it still flowed on as if things were fine.

Chapter 2 - RENFRO

The little town of Renfro, Pennsylvania rested in the northern Susquehanna River Valley. It was now a troubled place, but it had not always been so. It had once been a major junction for the Pennsylvania Railroad. Trains full of coal, iron ore, and lumber all traveled through Renfro until the 1960's, when the country had turned to the trucking industry for most of its transportation. During the Prohibition Era, trains from Renfro carried high quality Pennsylvania whiskey to Al Capone's clubs from New York to Chicago. During that era, the Renfro Station bustled with passenger trains as well. Residents could take daily trains to Harrisburg, Philadelphia, and New York City. Many immigrants who had gotten on trains in New

York ended up settling in the charming little mountain town of Renfro.

At that time, it was indeed charming, and there was plenty of work there. The people of Renfro were like most central Pennsylvanians though. They had an extreme fear of change. New ideas were usually viewed as bad ideas. This was a source of great frustration to Henry Newlen. Henry was head of the town council in the 1930's. Henry saw the need for change as Renfro grew and prospered. One evening, during a town meeting, his frustration reached a full boil. Henry was pleading with the council, and residents, to hire a policeman. Renfro had no law enforcement.

"Okay…Now look everybody," Henry began. "Our town is growin' and that's a good thing, but we're startin' to get the problems that come with growth. We need to think about a police officer for Renfro."

Most of the crowd groaned. They liked not having the eye of the law in town.

"Henry, you get goin' on this every month," Ben Keeler said. "What do we need a police officer for?"

Henry was determined to win them over.

"Well, take a look around!" Last month we had three traffic accidents, two cases of theft, I don't know how many drunk and dis-orderlies, and one case of a bad dog bite. We need somebody who can sort this stuff out legally."

"But Henry," Ben continued. "We can sort these problems out ourselves.

Janine Confer spoke up for Henry.

"I think Henry's right. Now, I don't know about all of you, but I, for one, am getting' tired of Darla Heggenstahler prancin' around wearin' practically nothin' but two band aids and a cork! I think she needs a few days in jail to cool off that fire she's got in her britches!"

Henry looked at Janine in a bit of confusion.

"Well now Janine, I appreciate your vote of support, but I'm not so sure that Darla's hot britches are a legal matter; although that girl IS bustin' out all over the place."

"Well, they should be!" Janine yelled.

"Well, if nobody has an objection, I could keep an eye on Darla," Shane Corbit said. Shane was a young, handsome logger, known for his "tomcat" ways.

The entire room laughed, except for Janine.

Janine mumbled, "Next thing, you'll be askin' Henry to have yer' pecker bronzed."

"All right," said Henry. "Let's get back to business. Now, please think about the problems we're havin.' We need some law. Now, let's have a vote. I vote "Yes" for lookin' for a police officer. Who's with me?"

Janine raised her hand, as she continued mumbling. However, she was the only one.

"OK," Henry sighed. "Well, let's move on to another issue. We need to think about a modern sewer system. Everybody in Renfro has a septic tank, and I think it's just a matter of time before the State requires us to have a sewer system for our town. We may as well get started on it now."

"I don't know Henry," Vern Glossner said. "I think ol' Jed Zuback needs the septic business. He gives us all a pretty good deal on takin' care of our septics."

"Well, even if we put a sewer system in town, there would still be plenty of business for Jed." Henry said with some frustration. "Now, look everybody! These changes are comin'. I think we at least need to start gettin' started with some preparations. They put in a sewer system down in Lockport, and it's real nice. Nobody has to have their septic hauled away now."

"But Henry, Lockport is twice the size of Renfro." Len Zerby stated. "We just don't need that kind a' thing yet."

"You're all missin' my point!" Henry's eyes were showing red. "We need to do some things to get ready. Our town is growin'. If we don't start getting' more comfortable with trying new ideas, it'll be the end of this town!"

Truer words had never been spoken. Henry was absolutely right. Good times would come to Renfro, and they would leave, for that very reason. Several industries built manufacturing facilities in Renfro, but labor problems forced them to close. Flooding along the Susquehanna River also caused problems. Industries informed the Renfro Town Council they would stay in the area if the city would build flood protection. The Renfro natives refused because they did not want to ruin the beauty of the river. So, more industries left town.

By the 1970's, when the railroad industry dried up, Renfro swiftly turned into a ghost town. Crime invaded in waves. Drug lords from New York City found they could use the isolated little town as a center for moving heroin. Pennsylvania's State Police were already spread far too thin to provide any regular law enforcement in the densely wooded area, so crime became rampant. Suddenly, the area was riddled with child abuse, drugs and even murder. Finally, the town council voted to hire a police officer and a part-time deputy.

The Renfro police chief was Warren Dale. He came from a long line of African American farmers who had left South Carolina to escape the Klan. Ezra Dale and his wife, Ella, rode the train north to Renfro around 1910. They found central Pennsylvanians to be only slightly less racist than whites in South Carolina, but the Dales were strong and stubborn. Ezra decided he was staying in Renfro, and nobody was going to move him. He and Ella started to farm tobacco, wheat and corn. In time, they established contacts with some of the more open-minded whites in Renfro, including the bootleggers of the Prohibition era. Ezra provided corn and grains for the whiskey distillers. They came to like dealing with Ezra because he kept his mouth shut, and provided them with quality ingredients, at a fair price, for their premium whiskey. In return, the bootleggers provided the Dales with protection from the Klan.

The king of the whiskey runners was Cooper McKivison, a tall handsome man, with a zest for life. He was over six feet tall, clean-shaven, with black flowing hair. He had seen his share of scrapes and had two scars on his face to prove it. He had a warm personality, and a great sense of humor, but he also had little tolerance for fools. Cooper came from a line of central Pennsylvania pastors. The McKivisons were the foundation of the Underground

Railroad in central Pennsylvania in the nineteenth century. Cooper left the calling to run whiskey during Prohibition. He had immediately taken a liking to Ezra and Ella and did everything he could to help them. One cold October night, Cooper knocked on the Dale's door.

"Evenin' Ezra. Hello Ella," he said politely. I don't want to alarm you two, but you need to stay in tonight, and make sure the doors are locked."

Ella's voice was calm, but quiet. She looked down at the shotgun Cooper held.

"What is it Cooper?"

Cooper gave her a warm reassuring smile.

"Oh, nothin' much Ella. Me and the boys have it all in hand. You both just stay put now"

Cooper turned and walked out the door. Ezra could see a large group of whiskey runners in his front yard. He knew what was about to happen, but he didn't dare tell his wife.

He gripped her hand and led her to the dining room table after locking the doors. Ezra sat down beside his wife and took out the large Bible they kept at the table. He began reading some of Ella's favorite passages.

Within minutes, about thirty Klansmen appeared, out of the darkness, behind the Dale farm. They wore the traditional sheets and carried a large wooden cross. Just as they planted the cross in the cold ground, and lit it, their eyes were blinded by the headlights of five pickup trucks. In the back of each truck were three moonshiners with shotguns.

"Well, look what we got here!" Cooper shouted. "I guess the general store must be clean outta' white sheets!"

Cooper stared at the chief Klansman at the front of the group.

"Is that you Devin Gurlach?" Cooper continued. "I shoulda' known, cuz' you're wearin' one o' them fitted sheets."

The moonshiners all laughed. The Klansman in front yelled to Cooper.

"We don't have no beef with you McKivison. We just want the nigger!"

Another Klansman spoke up.

"Get out a'the way McKivison! Give us the coon!" Without warning, Cooper took aim and shot down the burning cross with one shotgun blast. Before anyone could react, a trio of black cars came speeding in from out of nowhere, and parked in front of the Klansmen. The driver of one of the cars got out and quickly opened the back door.

The man who climbed out was wearing an expensive black suit, and an equally expensive fedora. He was not extremely tall, slightly heavy, and his round, boyish face looked almost pleasant. He had dark eyes, and a large scar on his left cheek. He swaggered with extreme confidence. He approached Cooper, as he looked at the Klansmen with a misleading smile. He patted Cooper on the back and stood beside him.

"Evening boys," he said. "Sorry I'm late. I just got off the train from New York…on my way back to Chicago."

The Klansmen turned and looked at one another with confusion. The man in the black suit continued.

"My main man Cooper here tells me we have a little problem with yous'. Is that right Coop?"

Cooper quietly answered.

"That's right Mr. Capone."

The Klan leader stiffened and took a step backward. Capone smiled again.

"Ya see boys. My man Ezra here…well, he's a big part of my operation. I got lots a' good people from New York to Chicago who really like my whiskey. And, well…Coop here, he tells me you boys is given' Ezra some grief."

After a silence, the Klan leader spoke up.

"We don't want no trouble Mr. Capone."

Capone whipped around and walked to the leader. He smiled and put his arm around the tall man in white.

"Well, now see? That's good! I like to hear that Devin!"

Devin Gurlach felt a lump in his throat at the realization that Al Capone knew his identity.

Capone patted Gurlach on the back and spoke again with a huge smile.

"See? Now we're getting' somewhere! Yeah! I think we're cookin' with spaghetti sauce now! Cuz, see

Devin…" Capone turned and spoke right into Gurlach's ear.

"See, you may have these fuckin' white sheets on, but the fact is…we know who all of you fucks are. And if I find out that yous' is messin' with my whiskey supply, then well…I'm not gonna' be happy. You understand Devin?"

Gurlach's voice was reduced to a whisper.

"I understand."

Capone was enjoying himself immensely. He threw his arms up as if singing an aria.

"All right! I think we've solved this little problem. Don't you Coop?"

"Yes sir, I do."

Capone looked back at the Klansmen.

"See boys, here's the thing. Yous' caught me in a good mood. I just had a nice hot meal on the train…a good glass a' wine, and a nice cigar. I feel good. Now, when I'm not in a good mood…well, things happen."

At that moment, the doors on the black cars opened and six more men in black suits got out. They all approached Capone and stood behind him. Capone lost his smile. His eyes seemed to slide back into his head as he glared at the group of white sheets.

"Let me tell you motherfuckers somethin'. I don't play no games with you country ass bastards. If you fuck with me, I'll find every one of ya'. You'll all be dead! I'll find your pretty country ass wives and kids, and they'll be dead! I'll throw your fuckin' white sheets in the river and I'll burn the country shacks yous' live in to the ground!"

Capone turned and nodded to one of his men. The man drew his gun and shot the Klansman closest to him in the head. The Klansman fell to the ground with scarlet blood spurting from the top of his white sheet. The Klansmen all took a step back. Several of Capone's men rushed forward, picked up the dead man, and threw him in the trunk of one of the cars. Cooper and his moonshiners still stood like statues with guns pointed. Capone walked over and again patted Cooper on the back. His wide smile returned.

"I'm SO glad we had this talk! I think we really took care of this little problem. I'd love to visit with yous', but wouldn't ya know it, I gotta' get back to Chicago. Hey! If you boys are ever there, look me up! Maybe we'll go to the opera. You country boys like opera?"

There was complete silence. Capone smiled, walked back to the car, and got in. In a matter of seconds, the cars were gone. Cooper spoke once more.

"Been a long night. Why don't you boys head home."

An owl hooted in a nearby tree, and the dry, dead leaves rustled along the ground, blown by an extra cold late October breeze. Without a sound, the white sheets disappeared into the night. Dale Farm never was visited by the Klan again.

Ezra and Ella tucked away every spare penny, and eventually enjoyed the largest and most productive farm in the region. Ezra's oldest son, Robert, saw that change was needed at the end of Prohibition. He began to convert farm land into grazing area for dairy cattle, and built large poultry barns. He and his younger brother, Roland, worked almost around the clock to build their dairy and egg farm into a successful business. Both men drove delivery trucks throughout central Pennsylvania mountain towns, when they weren't tending to cows and chickens. It was on one such delivery run that Roland met a beautiful African American woman by the name of Ida. After a long courtship, Roland and Ida married. At first, Robert had his doubts about his younger brother's bride. He thought Ida was too small and frail for farm life, and he feared she might leave Renfro due to the white supremacists there.

However, he soon found that inside her petite beauty was great strength and stubbornness. Ida fit right in to the way of life at Dale Farms. Robert never married. He claimed he was married to farming, and had no time for a wife.

One day, Robert was drilling a new water well with Chad Hiles. Chad was a big, strong farmer, who often helped Robert. He watched as Robert drilled deeper and deeper into the muddy pasture. Chad always had a plug of chew in his mouth. He had the amazing ability to work spitting into conversation.

"Hey Robert," he yelled over the drilling machinery. "Somethin' don't look right."

"What you talkin' about?" Robert yelled back.

"Well…I think the drill is shootin' back up out of the ground!"

"Huh?" Robert turned to look at the drill. His face snapped into an expression of shock.

"Sweet Jesus! Chad yelled. "We hit oil Robert!"

The two men ran back toward the farm as fast as they could as thick black oil erupted from the ground, tossing the drill bit high into the air.

"Holy shit, Robert! Chad continued after they were a safe distance back. "I never seen nothin' like that!"

"Me either," Robert said almost in a whisper, as he caught his breath from running.

The two men stood watching the oil shoot in a stream toward the sky. Black droplets fell onto their skin like rain.

"Hey Chad." Robert said quietly.

"Yeah?" Chad answered.

"I don't know how to cap no oil well, do you?"

"Nope." Chad answered. "What you gonna' do?"

Robert thought for a moment.

"Well…How about you get in the truck and go to the Western Union office. Mel Hawbaker down in Lockport has oil wells. Send him a telegram and tell him I'll pay him if he'll come up here an cap this…thing!"

It took a few days, but Mel did get the well capped. It was an added source of income for Dale farm. It was also an added source of contention for the Gurlach family, and other white supremacists in the area. Dale farm was prospering.

Chapter 3 - Warren Dale

As time passed, life on the Dale Farm continued in much the same manner. Many of the Renfro locals would stop at the farm each day for milk and eggs. Trucks would scatter to make deliveries; however, the deliveries now went to large stores and supermarkets instead of small country markets. It seemed that all Dales would continue to run the farm for an eternity until one day in 1985. That was the day when Warren Dale, then eight years-of-age ran into some trouble at Buckhorn Elementary School. Warren was minding his own business on the swings at recess, when Lucien Gurlach came strolling toward him. Lucien was a big kid, who was known for causing trouble. His family had been referred to as a "pack of hogs;" however, many people in Renfro felt that was an insult to hogs. Lucien was on his second trip through fifth grade, and many of the Buckhorn teachers were laying bets that he would succeed in going around a third time. It wasn't for a lack of intelligence. Lucien was indeed smart. He, and his family, simply despised authority of any kind. They had also been a thorn in the side of the Dale family for over eighty years.

"Hey nigger!" Lucien wailed. "That's my swing. Get off!"

"But I just got on it," Warren said patiently. "You can have it in a minute…and I'm not a nigger."

Lucien shoved Warren backwards into the mud, and gave out a loud belly laugh. Two of his equally "gifted" comrades laughed along with him and slapped Lucien on the back. As the three bullies enjoyed watching the youngster crawl out of the mud, Lucien was suddenly surprised by a hard slug to his stomach. He fell to the ground, writhing in pain, and holding his gut. The punch was thrown by Wesley McKivison, great grandson of the moonshiner, Cooper McKivison. Wesley was smart. He made sure a circle of his friends had surrounded him before he struck the blow, so no teachers would see what he had done.

"Really shouldn't pick on little kids Lucien," Wes said. "But I guess that makes you Gurlachs feel tough don't it!"

"You wait, McKivison! Lucien said. "We'll get you. We'll get you good you son of a bitch!"

"Yeah, right Gurlach. In yer' dreams!" Wes yelled over his shoulder.

Wes helped Warren back onto the swing.

"You ok Warren?" Wes calmly asked. "Don't worry. Them Gurlachs are all full of crap. You got as much right to that swing as any of us."

It was on that day that young Warren Dale decided he would become a police officer, rather than a farmer.

About a month later, the Gurlachs made good on Lucien's promise to get back at Wes. One day, as Wes walked alone along the river road, a pickup truck shot out of an old logging road and clipped him. He flew into the bushes, unconscious, as the truck sped off. He was later found by a truck driver, who called for an ambulance. Wes survived, but lost the use of his legs. He never got a look at the truck that hit him, or its driver, but everyone in Renfro knew it was one of the Gurlachs.

Chapter 4 – ASPEN

In 1992, in the city of Williamstown, Pennsylvania, Irene Winkleman was in the eighth month of a difficult pregnancy. The little boy she and her husband, Walt, were expecting was most active. Irene had suffered from severe morning sickness for the entire pregnancy, and had spent the past two months in bed. As she headed into the final month, she felt relief and peace. It was almost over. Soon, she and Walt would have a beautiful baby boy.

The day came when her doctor made the decision to opt for a Cesarean section birth. Now, as Irene laid waiting, with Walt holding her hand, she felt slightly uneasy. The doctor, and a crowd of nurses, stood around her, waiting, as the doctor prepared to introduce them to their little boy. His name would be Aspen Winkleman. The waiting was driving both Walt and Irene to the breaking point. At last, the doctor pulled the tiny baby out. Aspen peed mightily on the doctor's arm, but he did not cry. His eyes were large and full of surprise. The doctor and nurses assured Irene and Walt that the baby was fine, but still, he did not cry.

"Are you sure he's ok?" Irene called out.

At last, Aspen let out a cry as he was placed on the table at the side of the room. Irene and Walter sighed in relief. They had a healthy baby boy. The wait was over. As the doctor returned to caring for Irene, the nurses gently handed Aspen to his father. Walt carried his son down the long corridor to the nursery. He looked down at Aspen's face, and felt his eyes well up with tears of joy.

"Hey little buddy," Walt cooed. "Your name is Aspen Winkleman."

Aspen looked up at his dad. His huge eyes hardly blinked as Walt carried him. Walt watched as the nurses gently wrapped Aspen in a blanket and placed a tiny knitted stocking cap on his head. Again, Aspen didn't cry until he was placed in the crib in the nursery. The nurses told Walt that was normal, and suggested that he return to Irene. Walt looked back at his son in the crib again before returning to his wife. The wait was over... a perfect little boy! Before returning to Irene, Walt sat for a moment in the dark waiting room, and felt gentle, warm tears of joy rolling down his weary face. He said a short prayer of thanks, and slowly walked back to Irene in the delivery room.

The next day, a nurse carried Aspen in to see Irene. Aspen was still crying and had done so most of the night. The weary nurse asked Irene if she would hold Aspen to see if that would stop his crying. As soon as Aspen was nestling beside Irene, the crying immediately stopped. Irene was still hooked up to machines, and was receiving pain killers, but she didn't mind having Aspen asleep at her side. In fact, she wanted him close to her. Aspen stayed with her for the rest of the hospital stay. Every time the nurses tried to take him back to the nursery, the screaming began again. Tiny Aspen was already making his mark on the world.

As Aspen matured, he showed great interest in colorful toys. He began to make the usual baby "cooing" noises. He loved to sit in his swing and rock slowly. In fact, the swing was the only way to get him to take a nap. He stared into his dad's face as he drank his evening bottle before bed. He loved formula, and he slept all through the night. Formula had become necessary because it was discovered that Irene was anemic, and had developed mastitis. She had a fever, her breasts ached, and she felt weak and tired.

"It will be all right. We will get through this," she thought to herself. "Walt is strong, and I'll get better."

In fact, things did get better. Irene recovered. Walt returned to work, and life seemed to be going well for the Winkleman family. Then, Irene began to have doubts as she watched Aspen. At first, she said nothing to Walt, but she noticed Aspen seemed to be distant from her. One day, as he crawled on the floor, she called to him.

"Here Aspen! Come to momma!" she called.

Aspen did not even return her gaze. She called to him again, a bit louder. Still, he did not seem to notice.

"Oh God no! He's deaf!" Irene cried out.

She clapped her hands sharply. Aspen jumped at the sound and started to cry. Irene picked him up and consoled him, half laughing because he could hear her, and half crying because she was still afraid. Just like in the hospital, he cried and cried, until Irene cradled him in her arms, much as he had been cradled in her tummy during pregnancy.

"Oh God! What's wrong with my Aspen?" Irene cried as she watched her baby gazing into her eyes.

As the first year ended, Aspen entertained himself by watching the television. He and Irene watched public television each morning. Irene held him next to her, and tried to interact with him, but found that his focus was completely on the television. She would finally turn it off in the late morning. This led to major tantrums. Aspen would scream, flap his hands, and cry huge duct tears. Sometimes, he would also throw things across the room, and at her. Finally, after she thought she would lose her mind from Aspen's screams, Irene would turn the television back on. The fits would immediately stop, but Aspen would return to gazing at the television in a stupor. Finally, with her nerves shot, Irene felt she had to tell Walt.

"He's too quiet," she told Walt. "He just seems to "zone out."

"Maybe he's just content." Walt would reply.

When he was in his crib, Aspen would often stare at the mobile over his bed, to the point of not noticing anything else, even loud noises like thunder, or fire sirens.

Walt was too exhausted to notice. He fell into a deep sleep, and relished the fact that Aspen was so quiet. However, Irene was becoming frantic. She prayed that her son would come out of his silent little universe.

Finally, at around eighteen months, Aspen began to make some small sounds…not words, but they sounded like music to Irene. Maybe her son was finally starting to develop normally. She worked tirelessly with her son during the day. She read books to him, and conversed with him, until she couldn't think of anything else to say. Occasionally, to her delight, Aspen would repeat a word she had spoken. Then, on one magical day, she heard Aspen watching his favorite show. There was a song playing, and he was singing along with it! She cried tears of joy and hugged Aspen, as she praised him. When Walt came home, she put the DVD back on, and played it. Again, Aspen began singing along. Walt picked him up and hugged his little boy.

Things continued in this manner for months. Aspen would talk to the television, but not to people. Then, around age two, Aspen once again grew silent. The singing stopped. When he played, he took great care to line up his cars, trucks, and blocks in perfect lines, arranged neatly by color. He sat silently for hours at a time. Irene would try reading to him, but he would pull away, and return to organizing his toys. He would use his crayons to re-create, with excellent detail, scenes from his favorite television shows, but the singing and babbling had completely stopped. Aspen was once again completely immersed in his tiny, silent world.

"That's it Walt!" Irene screamed in panic. "Goddamit! We're taking him to a doctor! Something is wrong!"

Walt finally agreed. He and Irene called the doctor the next day. After the appointment, they were given a referral to a child developmental specialist. Aspen was given a full evaluation, and diagnosis. He was autistic. Irene was devastated. Walt felt shock, but he did his best to remain strong for Irene.

Walt took time off from work to spend more time helping with Aspen. Irene was showing signs of mental and physical stress. She had great difficulty sleeping, and blamed herself for Aspen's autism. Walt tried his best to console her, and put her guilt to rest. It was ineffective. She got colds all the time, and frequently suffered from flu-like symptoms.

When Aspen was three, Walt and Irene agreed to try sending him to a morning pre-school program that included children with developmental disabilities. Walt desperately needed to return to work. He was completely out of vacation and sick days. He also felt that Irene might benefit from having mornings free to rest.

Aspen began to show tremendous development in a short time. He began talking… slowly, at first. However, after a few months of being around the other children, his speech began to flow non-stop. In fact, he began to sound like a professor of English, pouring out long words that no small child should know. He loved to spend time on computers. He began to read books at an alarming rate. Most of all, Aspen developed some fascinating super-human abilities. He was very perceptive of human emotions, even when those around him said nothing. He was especially aware of anger and sadness and would sometimes burst into tears of empathy if he sensed someone in the room was sad. However, Aspen's greatest ability was indeed supernatural. He regularly saw and spoke with spirits of the dead. One day, as she heard a lengthy conversation Aspen was having in the living room, Irene went in to praise her son, thinking he was talking to the television. Instead, Aspen informed her that he was talking to Grandpa Homer.

"Honey...Grandpa died years ago."

"I am aware of that," Aspen said with attitude. "But he was just here with me."

These visits from the dead also included family pets. Aspen had regular visits from Beasley, the family basset hound, who had died the previous year. Aspen would giggle as he flopped on the couch. When Irene asked him why he was laughing, he would report,

"Beasley is licking my face!"

One evening, Irene was looking at an old ring given to her by her grandmother just before her death. Aspen took it from her, looked at his mother and said,

"Great Grandma says the diamond ring is missing a prong."

After examining the ring, Irene indeed found that one of the prongs around the large diamond stone was missing. She had never noticed this before.

Simultaneously, Aspen developed some small quirks. He was extremely uncomfortable around anything that flew...bees, birds, and butterflies all caused him to duck and run. He disliked crowded, loud rooms, but had an amazing ability to pick out, and listen to, a conversation going on between two people in a crowd. He could recall anything he had seen, down to the smallest detail. For example, he could draw, from memory, a building he had seen down to the correct number of windows and doors. The sound of a freight train didn't bother him, but the sound of Irene's hair dryer caused him to cover his ears and scream.

It was time for kindergarten. Aspen did well in school. He was extremely bright, but also a bit awkward. He refused to color at his desk. He preferred to color on the floor under it. He carefully lined up his carrots at lunch before he ate them and asked for toothpicks to pick up any messy food, like pickles. Eventually, Irene packed toothpicks daily in his lunch box.

Walt shared his love of the outdoors with his son. He and Aspen spent countless hours at the park. Aspen loved to sit in the tire swing as Walt pushed him in the warm sun. This relaxed him so much that he would occasionally start to drift off and Walt would catch him just before he fell from the swing. Aspen loved to go to the park after a rain to look for worms on the damp sidewalk. He would gently lift the worms from the blacktop and place them in the wet grass. One day, after moving worms for almost an hour, it was getting dark. Aspen became distressed. He wanted to keep moving worms, but Walt said they had to go. Aspen began to cry. The cry grew to a scream, and the scream became a fit. Walt tried to console his little boy.

"Aspen…We have to get home. It's getting dark." Walt started to pat Aspen's head, then realized touching his son only prolonged the fits. He squatted down by Aspen and spoke quietly.

"Hey, buddy. I'm sorry, but we just can't save all the worms after it rains."

Aspen continued crying for several minutes, but eventually began to de-escalate. Finally, after Walt promised they would come back the next day, Aspen took his father's hand and left the park.

As the years passed, Aspen excelled in school. He was placed in honors classes in middle school and high school. He became an expert in computer programming, math, science and literature. Reading was one of his greatest loves. He read Homer's ODYSSEY and loved it. He played chess for the high school chess club, and always won.

Irene; however, did not fare well as the years passed. She was riddled with guilt over Aspie's autism. She fell into depression often.

"If I'd just eaten healthier foods, and exercised more, maybe this wouldn't have happened!" she cried to Walt.

No matter what Walt tried, he could not rid Irene of her guilt. Trips to a therapist had helped her a bit, but her depression did not improve. She began to have severe joint and muscle pain. Her doctors ran more tests and prescribed strong pain killers, but still her pain worsened.

After months of medical tests, Irene found that she suffered from lupus. In fact, her doctor informed her that she had probably had it since her teen years but didn't know it. Lupus was so difficult to diagnose, her physician had said, that many people only found out later in life that they had it. Often, a trauma to the body, such as childbirth, would trigger an onset of more severe symptoms. Irene's depression became unbearable as her lupus advanced. She retreated to bed, despite her doctor's warnings that doing so would make her condition worse. Her lupus overtook her brain. She began to hallucinate. Walt was exhausted. He was caring for Irene and Aspie when he arrived home each evening. He began to fear that Irene would fall and hit her head, or possibly even take her own life. He hired a nurse to be with Irene while he was at work. One night, after a particularly grueling day, Walt was sitting with her. She was in a panic and couldn't catch her breath. Walt gave her an extra dose of morphine to calm her. The nurse had told him to do so if necessary. Walt sat and gently held her hand. He told her how much he and Aspen loved her, hoping she would relax and fall asleep. She smiled and said,

"I love you both."

Irene closed her eyes and drifted off into sleep. Walt held her hand for a moment longer, then took the morphine back to the refrigerator. He checked on Aspie as he slept. When he returned to Irene's room, she had passed away in peaceful slumber.

Aspen was 17 when Irene died. He accepted her death well. He missed their talks. He had always been able to discuss books with Irene, since she had a deep love of literature. In her last months, Aspen read to her every day; however, he had also started to dislike going into her room. Seeing her so sick gave him an uneasy, painful feeling. He had started to tell Walt that he did want to go into "the sick room" every day.

Aspen and Walt moved to an apartment after Irene's death. It was affordable and comfortable. Caring for Irene had taken a toll on Walt. His eyes always looked sad, even when he smiled. He had back problems from lifting Irene and dressing her daily. Fortunately, their townhouse was conveniently located. Walt was only a few blocks from his office, and he enjoyed walking to work. Aspen could catch the city bus to go to work at the local library, where he worked shelving books, and maintaining the library computers. He had begun this job after high school. He often finished his work quickly and was able to pursue his greatest passion…reading. Their life was simple, but most pleasant. They had a cat named Norman, a grey and black tabby. Norman and Aspie were inseparable. They read together, slept together, and much to Walt's disapproval, ate together.

Life continued in this manner for several years for Walt and Aspen. It was a good time. Walt eventually retired. He and Aspen enjoyed their time together. They ate at their favorite restaurants, went to movies, and took long, relaxing walks together.

The West Branch of the Susquehanna River flows like a shimmering snake through much of Pennsylvania. Walt and Aspen's new home was only a block from Riverview Park. They spent countless hours walking in the park. It was especially beneficial for Walt. He loved the peace of the river. One day, as he and Aspen walked, Walt stopped and stared, with a gentle smile, at the ducks on the river.

"Look Aspen," he said. "The ducks are so content. They are so happy floating in the river. They are simply happy, just being ducks."

Aspen looked at the ducks, and then at Walt. He was concerned that Walt was obsessing so on the ducks.

Walt continued, "Wouldn't it be wonderful if people could just be content to be who they are…floating through life, just like those ducks are floating in the river. People think they need so many things to be happy…but they don't. They just need to flow with the river."

Aspen was getting worried. He put his arm on his dad's shoulder, something he almost never did. Aspen did not like to touch others or show affection. However, he could feel his dad's need for compassion. He gently guided Walt along the path toward home.

As he grew older, Aspen's psychic abilities sharpened. He frequently handed Walt's phone to him seconds before it would ring. He would be in the middle of a book and would suddenly call to Walt that someone was at the door. Seconds later, the doorbell would ring.

One morning, Aspen awoke to a quiet house. Normally, he could hear Walt making breakfast for the two of them and smell the coffee brewing. He walked downstairs. The townhouse was dark.

"Dad?" Aspen called?

He had a deep feeling of darkness. Something was wrong.

Aspen went upstairs to his father's room. He opened the door slowly.

"Dad?"

Aspen froze. He saw Walt's lifeless body still in bed. Walt was pale. His mouth hung open, but his eyes were closed peacefully. Aspen felt for a heartbeat. There was none. He ran to his room and got his phone. After dialing 911, he began to feel the terror of the moment. He knew he was alone now…on his own forever.

Chapter 5 - TWO WORLDS MEET

As Aspen rode in the Williamstown Police car, with Officer Ryan Mays, he looked at the beautiful Susquehanna River, shimmering in the sunlight. Aspen had been called upon to assist Warren Dale, in Renfro, with finding Emily McKivison. Officer Mays was fond of Aspen and had offered to drive him up the river road to the tiny mountain town.

"Now, Aspen…You need to work with Chief Dale on this case," Mays said. "He's a good man, and I think you're gonna' like him. He has a nice farm and his wife, Sherry, is really sweet.

"Are there chickens on the farm?" Aspen asked with some fear in his voice.

"Chickens…well, yeah, I suppose there are. Now Aspen, I know you don't like birds, and things that fly, but don't worry about that."

"I despise chickens." Aspen replied.

Mays went on.

"Aspen, this is a real important case. Nobody has been able to find this girl, and I think you can help."

Aspen went back to looking at the river. He wore his standard clothing…jeans, perfectly white sneakers, and a blue rain slicker with a hood. He was always prepared for rain that way.

As the police cruiser approached Renfro, Aspen could hardly believe the way the houses teetered on the mountain sides in the deep valley. They looked as if they might topple downhill, and into the river at any minute. Finally, the car pulled into Dale Farms. Chief Warren was waiting with his wife, Sherry, to greet their guest. Warren remembered the phone call from his friend Ryan Mays.

"Now, Warren…Aspen is a little quirky. He's autistic, and well…you might notice a few, uh…unusual ways he has about him."

"That's ok," Warren responded. "I'm kinda' used to quirky in THIS town."

"Well," Ryan continued. "He's got some REALLY quirky ways. For example, he hates anything that flies."

Warren asked, "You mean he doesn't like to go on planes?"

"Uh, no," Officer Mays struggled to explain. "He hates birds, bugs, bats…you know. Things that fly really bother him. So, you might notice he's a little uneasy around your chickens. See what I mean?"

"Oh. Okay," Dale said. "I guess we can handle that."

Ryan broke in. "And he eats with toothpicks a lot. He likes his food nice and neat, see? And he scrubs his white shoes every single night to keep 'em nice and white, and he also always wears a blue rain slicker, just in case it rains, and..."

"Okay! Okay!" Dale had heard enough. "I get it. He's got quirks. I'll tell Sherry about the toothpicks."

Warren put the phone call out of his head for the moment, as the car pulled in. He needed all the help he could find with this case.

Ryan pulled to a stop by Warren and Sherry. He got out, smiling, and shook Warren's hand. Sherry greeted him with a warm hug, as they exchanged pleasantries.

When the three of them turned around, Aspen was still in the car. He looked terrified. Chickens and large white ducks had come running, in hope of a meal, when the car had pulled in. Aspen had pulled up the hood on his blue raincoat and had his hands over his ears.

"Oh, uh...here. Let me chase away the birds," Mays said. "Aspen really don't like birds."

He chased the flock back toward the barn. Very slowly, Aspen lowered his hood, and surveyed the area. When he felt it was safe, he slowly opened the car door and got out.

He straightened his raincoat, and jeans, while looking down at his feet. He was concerned about his perfectly white shoes in the farm mud. Finally, he looked up, and made eye contact with the Dales.

"Uh...Aspen," Ryan said. "This is Chief Warren Dale, and his wife, Sherry."

Dale reached out his big hand to shake, but Aspen slowly extended his clenched fist.

"Bump please," Aspen said.

Dale was confused.

"Huh?"

"Oh…I forgot to tell ya' Warren," Mays stated. "Aspen don't like to shake hands…germs and all, you know. He does knuckle bumps."

Warren closed his hand into a fist. Aspen gently bumped knuckles. Sherry was moving toward Aspen with arms extended for a warm hug. Aspen stepped back and gave out a tiny whimper.

Mays soothed her.

"Oh, uh Sherry. I'm sorry. Aspen is a little funny about hugs and being touched."

"Bump please," Aspen said again with his fist extended.

Sherry was slightly confused, but she responded with a short bump of knuckles.

"Well," Warren said. "Aspen…Let's get you settled in your room."

Just as Warren completed his sentence, Aspen grabbed a huge suitcase from the trunk of the car and placed it in the Chief's hand. The case was so heavy, Dale lost his grip on it, and it fell onto his foot, with a crashing sound.

"Thank you, Chief Dale," Aspen said with little emotion, as he followed Sherry into the house.

Sherry showed Aspen to his room. A few minutes later, Warren finally reached the top of the stairs with the immense bag Aspen had handed him.

"Well, Aspen," Sherry said. "We'll let you get settled."

"That would be nice," Aspen responded in a business-like tone. "Thank you."

That evening at dinner, Aspen sat at the head of the table. He carefully arranged his carrots in a row. He asked Sherry to please place his mashed potatoes in a bowl, with no gravy, and he cut his boneless chicken breast into tidy squares. He examined his silverware closely before deciding it was sanitary. He took a tiny corner of the chicken cube in his front teeth and nibbled at it. It was safe to eat. Finally, after chewing his first bite twenty times exactly, he spoke.

"This is delicious, Sherry! You know, I enjoy cooking. I'm curious. How do you give your breasts such a soft texture?"

Sherry raised her eyebrows slightly, but only for a second. She had been well prepared for Aspen's quirks.

"Oh, it's all in how you handle 'em," Warren said, with a hearty laugh.

"Thank you, Aspen. I'm glad you like it," Sherry said, as she smiled, and took a playful slap at her husband. "I make the chicken tender by marinating it in honey mustard and lemon juice."

Aspen looked at Warren.

"Did you kill this chicken, Chief Dale?"

"Uh, no, Aspen. My brother, Thomas did. He does most of the farm work now. I just help when I can."

"Oh," Aspen replied.

He thought for a moment.

"When I was little, I used to think they shot chickens. I thought there were many men with guns at chicken farms, who went around shooting the chickens."

Aspen laughed uproariously at his statement. Warren and Sherry sat, looking at one another, with slight grins. Finally, Aspen stopped laughing and took another bite.

At the end of dinner, Sherry asked Aspen if he would like some dessert…cherry pie.

"Oh, no thank you Sherry," he replied. "Cherries give me terrible flatulations. I'm quite tired. I think I'll go to my room to sleep now."

"It's only a little before seven, Aspen," Warren said. "What time do you like to get up?"

"About four-thirty," Aspen responded.

"Oh, I see," Warren stated. "Well, we get up around six, so maybe you want to, uh…"

"Oh, I like to jog every morning," Aspen interrupted. "I think tomorrow, I'll jog through town and look around."

"Oh, that's a good idea," Sherry said. "I'll have breakfast ready for you when you get back."

"Oh, I'll need a long shower first. I sweat profusely," Aspen responded.

Aspen bid them good night and retreated to his room.

Aspen got up promptly at 4:30. It was chilly, so he wore his grey sweatpants, and sweatshirt. He wiped off his white sneakers and put on his standard blue rain slicker. He tied the house key Warren had given him the night before to his wrist, and quietly slipped out the door. The chickens were loose and wandered around the back porch. Aspen froze for a moment, not sure of how to avoid them. He began to flail his arms and make barking sounds. The chickens dispersed and he was on his way.

As he ran down Dale Lane, he passed the pasture where an oil well still worked. He passed rows of poultry barns, and finally came to the dairy cattle barn. Thomas was already at work getting the cows milked. He waved to Aspen.

"Hello!" Aspen called.

When Aspen turned toward town on the river road, he could hear the Susquehanna, flowing nearby. It was soothing. He remembered hearing that sound when walking

by the river water with his father years ago. He jogged

along the old railroad buildings that seemed to go on for

miles. They were empty and run-down now. He tried to

picture them during the railroad boom, when they were full

of life. He jogged into town. There were a few lights on,

but most of the town was incredibly dark. There were only

a few street lights. Suddenly, something very large and

dark appeared in front of him. Aspen stopped. He could

barely make it out in the black of early morning. Then, he

heard it make a grunting sound. It knocked over a trash can,

and Aspen immediately realized it was a huge black bear!

He had seen a nature program about bears, and he

remembered that if one encountered a bear, the best thing

to do was hold still, with both arms straight out.

Supposedly, this made one look bigger, and the bear would

move on. So, Aspen stood…arms out, and eyes shut tightly.

It seemed like he stood there for hours. Finally, he opened

one eye. He sighed in relief. The bear was gone. He decided it might be best to start back to the farm. He smiled and turned around. There was the bear, staring him in the face! It had silently moved behind him, as he stood with his arms out, and eyes closed. Aspen screamed like a small child.

"Braaaaaahhhhhhh!!!!!

The bear also screamed, turned around, and headed for the woods behind a house. Aspen took off like a shot, running faster than he ever had in the opposite direction from the bear. He shot past the railroad buildings, down the river road, and back to the house. He screamed at the chickens and they all parted like the Red Sea. Aspen ran between all the chickens and into the house. Sherry was up and was making coffee.

"Good morning, Aspen," she said, as Aspen dashed through the kitchen.

Aspen shot up the stairs, into his room, and slammed the door. Warren cautiously walked out of the bathroom, and knocked gently on Aspen's door.

"You OK, Aspen?"

After a brief silence, Aspen spoke.

"Oh yes. Thank you. I'll be down for breakfast in a few minutes."

"Okay," Warren answered. He shook his head a little in bewilderment and started downstairs.

Later that morning, Warren was going over the Emily McClintock case with Aspen.

"She simply disappeared into thin air after school one day," Warren said. "Nobody saw her after she left the school grounds."

"How old is she?" Aspen inquired.

"Sixteen…model student, babysits kids all over town, National Honor Society."

Aspen held Emily's phone in his hand. It was the only possession of hers that had been recovered. It had been found on the road by the high school. Aspen often got information from holding onto someone's possession. He wasn't getting much psychic information from Emily's phone, but he did not have the feeling a foreboding he had gotten before, from holding a possession of someone who had been murdered.

"I do not think Emily is dead. Who found this phone?"

"Emily's mom. She went looking for her at the school."

Aspen sat and thought for a moment. He held the phone a little longer. Still, nothing came to him.

"Chief Dale," Aspen said. "Could you take me to see some places that Emily liked to go?"

"Sure," Warren replied. "We can start with the diner. One of Emily's friends works there. Her name is Katy Rosamilia."

Warren and Aspen headed into Renfro in the squad car. It was an old Ford with a huge engine. The town had purchased it at an auto auction. Aspen looked around at the worn interior. His thin body looked somewhat comical in the huge bench seat in the front, with a shotgun mounted at his side. The engine roared like a stock car, causing Aspen to squint at the noise.

They arrived at the Renfro Diner around mid-morning. It was quiet now that the breakfast hour was over. There were a few coffee drinkers sitting at the old-fashioned counter, but the tables were empty.

"Hello Warren!" One old-timer said, over his cup of coffee.

"Hey Derek," Warren answered. "How are ya'?"

"Oh...no complaints. Don't do no good anyway. How's Sherry?"

"She's fine Derek. Is Katy workin' today?"

"I'm here Warren," a young woman answered as she came out of the kitchen door.

Dale continued. "Hey Katy. Got a minute?"

"Sure," the young woman said, as she walked over.

"Katy," Warren said. "This is Aspen Winkleman. He's from Williamstown. Aspen's come up here to help us with Emily's case.

"Oh," she said. "Are you a policeman?"

"No," Dale said. "Aspen is a psychic. He's helped the police in Williamstown solve some missing person cases, and well, they thought he might be able to help us."

Aspen nodded, "Hello...Katy."

"Hello."

Aspen was smitten. Katy was beautiful. In fact, he lowered his hood on his blue slicker and attempted to straighten his hair. Katy had short brown hair, and an angelic face. Her eyes were brown and inviting. Her skin was light brown from her Italian ancestry. Although simply dressed in jeans, a t-shirt, and an apron, she looked dazzling. However, it was her personal warmth that struck Aspen most. Katy transmitted a true feeling of love, and nurturing toward others. He hadn't experienced it since his early years, when his mother had been in better health.

"Hey Warren," Derek called. "Come on over here and have a cup a' joe with me.

Dale looked at Katy and Aspen.

"OK Derek," he called. "I'm comin'. Why don't you and Aspen talk a while, Katy. Maybe you can give him some info on Emily that will help."

"OK," Katy answered.

Dale went over to Derek and some of the other old-timers. He poured a cup of coffee from the old Bunn coffee maker and sat down.

"So…Aspen," Katy said, with a beautiful smile. "You're a psychic?"

Aspen was incredibly nervous. He had never felt this way about a woman before. He felt sweat on his palms, and there was a slight rushing in his ears. He struggled to say something.

"Yes…that is correct. You see, I'm autistic, and I have some psychic abilities that others do not. Uh…I used to see my dead dog, Beasley, quite a bit…and my dead grandparents…"

Aspen felt panic. He cleared his throat.

"Oh no," he thought. "That was stupid!"

"Wow!" Katy answered, to his surprise. "That's really interesting."

Katy leaned, just a bit, across the table toward Aspen. Aspen began to relax. The sweat was no longer making his palms slick, and his heart slowed down a little.

"Katy," he said. "You were good friends…I mean…You ARE good friends with Emily?"

"Yeah. I was kind of like her big sister. She would come in almost every day to see me here."

Katy wasn't intimidated by Aspen's quirks. In fact, she felt completely at ease with him.

"Was there anyone who hated…uh, I'm sorry. Was there anyone who maybe did not like Emily very much?"

Katy didn't hesitate.

"Everyone seemed to love her. I can't think of anyone who would want to hurt her. I mean, we have some bad people here, but Emily always minded her own business, and never seemed to have enemies."

Aspen continued. "Who can you think of who is a bad person?"

"Well," Katy said carefully. "There are a quite a few people around here who hate just about everyone. Warren can tell you all about them."

Aspen looked around. He noticed a small cluster of men around Warren. They were all laughing and enjoying themselves; however, there were a few people who remained far away, and had nothing to do with Warren.

"Emily loved kids, and she loved doing good things for people," Katy said. "I still can't think of any reason someone would have to hurt her."

A couple of customers walked in. Katy motioned for them to have a seat.

"I have to get back to work now, Aspen," Katy said.

"Yes, thank you for talking to me," Aspen replied.

Katy smiled and headed back toward the kitchen. Before she went through the door, she turned and smiled at Aspen. She gave a little wave, and disappeared.

Warren and Aspen returned to the squad car. They took off on a tour of Renfro. Aspen had never seen so many old, deteriorating buildings. It was clear that Renfro had once been a busy place. As they drove toward the old airplane factory, they passed two men. One glared at the squad car, and at Warren. The other, younger man walked with an unusual shuffle. Aspen watched him carefully. He saw the man begin to flap his hands. He knew immediately that the man was autistic.

"Chief...Who are those men?" Aspen inquired.

"Oh Lord, Aspen," Warren said with a deep sigh. "That nasty looking guy is Lucien Gurlach. He's about the baddest S.O.B. around here. That little guy with him is his poor brother, Owen. Owen has…well, he has lots of disabilities."

"Yes," Aspen continued. "I am quite sure Owen is autistic, as I am. Why did the other man, Lucien, look at us with so much anger?"

Warren shook his head. "Well…it goes back a very long way, Aspen. The Gurlach family has always had a problem with anybody…different."

"Do you mean they have a problem with African Americans, like you?" Aspen asked.

"Yeah, and just about anybody who isn't like them. But, especially people who aren't white. Sad fact, Aspen…There's lots of folks around here who are just like old Lucien there. In fact, he's the reason I became a cop, instead of a farmer. In school, Lucien used to bully me all the time. The Gurlach family has been giving my family grief for almost a hundred years."

"Warren…Does Lucien break the law?"

"Yeah, Aspen…the Gurlachs run heroin, and do just about everything bad you can imagine. Problem is catching them. I'd love to put Lucien away for a long time, but I've never been able to catch him in the act. He has lots of other people who work for him, and cover for him, cuz' they're scared of him. I've caught plenty of his helpers, but he always manages to keep his distance, and let the others take the heat. You hardly ever see Lucien in town. Most of the time, he's out there in the mountains. He's hard to find."

Aspen quietly asked, "Do you think it is possible Lucien took Emily?"

"I had him at the station for two hours, Aspen," Warren replied. "The State Troopers and I interrogated him, and then we called him back for another two hours and got nothing. The problem is, we got a bunch of other people in these parts who also could have taken Emily."

The squad car was now heading out the river road away from town. The river sparkled. It looked so tranquil, yet it flowed through what Aspen now realized, was a very troubled town. Warren pulled into a driveway at an old house that rested just a short distance from the calm Susquehanna.

"This is Jess McKivison's house," Warren said. "I think you might want to talk with her…maybe look at Emily's room. Maybe you'll get some, you know…information or feelings or somethin'"

When Jess McKivison came to the door, Aspen felt immediate sorrow. It didn't take someone with psychic abilities to see the pain this woman was feeling. Her face was pale and drawn, as if she hadn't slept in weeks. She was beyond thin. Aspen thought she resembled a holocaust survivor he had seen in a photo. She held a cup of coffee in one hand, and a cigarette in the other. Warren spoke softly.

"Hi Jess. Sorry to bother you, but this is Aspen. I think he may be able to help us."

Jess tried to smile. Her lips barely moved as she uttered a tiny "hello" at Aspen.

"Hello, Jess," Aspen said quietly. "Is it possible for me to come in and look around? It might help me acquire some information about Emily. I have some Psychic abilities."

Aspen's voice lacked his usual straight, autistic sound. He had always been able to feel pain in others. He had mastered speaking with comfort when he read to his sick mother years earlier.

Jess seemed to feel a small surge of energy. Perhaps it was due to the chance Aspen might be able to lead them in a positive direction. She motioned for them to come inside. Little Abe was staying with other members of the McKivison family during the day, to try and give Jess a rest, and to protect him from the anguish she was feeling.

Aspen began to look around the living room. Jess had the drapes closed, so it was dark. He slowly looked around.

"Do you mind if I pick up some things and hold them for a minute?" Aspen asked. "Sometimes I get information from objects."

"No, please…go ahead," Jess almost whispered.

Aspen picked up several objects but got nothing.

"May I please go to Emily's room?"

Jess led him upstairs. Emily's door was closed. Jess had shut it the day Emily disappeared, and had not looked in it since. She opened the door, but still could not look inside the room. Aspen gently passed her and began looking around. He picked up some dolls…nothing. He placed his hand on some of her personal objects…a hairbrush, a hand mirror. Still, he got nothing. He picked up her pillow. He didn't get any feeling from it, but he noticed a large crack in the wall behind Emily's bed. Carefully, he reached inside. He felt something. It was a book, hidden in the wall. Aspen pulled it out, and realized he was holding Emily's diary. He didn't open it. He held it tightly in his hands.

As soon as Aspen felt the book, a rush of pictures flooded his mind. He saw Emily, this girl he had never met. He saw her face clearly.

"Chief Dale," Aspen exclaimed, with some excitement. "Please come here!"

Warren and Jess almost knocked Aspen over, as they ran toward him.

"It's Emily's diary!" Warren said. "How'd we miss that?"

"Jess?" Aspen asked. "Does Emily have strawberry blonde hair, and glasses?"

"Yes!" Jess almost yelled with excitement. "Can you see her?"

Aspen's eyes were now closed. He was immersed in a trance. He returned to his autistic voice and began reciting.

"I see Emily with a little boy. They are playing in the yard. There is a dog…a beagle."

"That's my folks' dog, Rocky," Jess exclaimed.

Aspen went on.

"There are balloons, and other children. It's a party, and Jess is playing hide and seek with the children. She is counting while the children hide. There is a white cake on a picnic table. The adults at the party are playing horseshoes. Oh no! A thunderstorm. Everyone is running inside."

Aspen stopped. He was sweating and seemed to be exhausted. His breathing was slightly labored.

"That's all I'm getting…Jess," he said. "Could you please get me some water?"

"Of course! Aspen, you just described Abe's last birthday party perfectly…and you didn't even open the book!"

"Yes," Aspen answered. "I saw many images."

"I'll get your water," Jess said.

Jess ran from the room. A strangeness came over her. She hadn't felt this way in weeks. As she ran downstairs, she realized she was feeling hope.

Warren went over to Aspen, who was trying to calm down. He was sitting in a chair by the window.

"Aspen," he said. "Are you ok?"

"Yes, Chief," Aspen responded, still short of breath.

"You just relax. Jess is getting you some water."

"Chief," Aspen continued. "I do not really need water. I just wanted Jess to leave the room. I must tell you something."

"What is it?" Warren asked.

Aspen listened for a moment to make sure Jess was not close by.

"After holding Emily's diary," Aspen said. "I'm quite sure that she is still alive."

Jess returned with the water.

"Jess," Warren said. "We really need to keep Emily's diary. Aspen and I will go through it for anything that might help us."

"Sure!" Jess said, as she briefly managed a smile.

Aspen and Warren spent the rest of the afternoon combing over Emily's diary entries. Most of them were typical teenage girl diary entries...boys she liked, thoughts about her favorite music, and books she loved. However, there were several vague entries about one of her friends, Jacob Meyers. Emily constantly wrote in her diary that Jacob was very troubled and needed help, but she didn't go into detail. Some of her entries about the young man seemed indicate fear.

"Do you know this young man, Jacob?" Aspen asked.

"Yeah," Warren answered. "He's a good kid. He's real quiet, and seems to be a good student, but he keeps to himself. I don't think he has any friends except Emily."

"Perhaps we should speak with him," Aspen stated.

The two men got into the old squad car, and headed to the Myers' home. It was late afternoon, and the sun was sinking low behind the trees. The river glowed with silver and grey from the light and dark patches of clouds, scattered throughout the sky. Central Pennsylvanians were most familiar with cloudy weather that moved into the area, and stayed for days, or weeks. As they drove, a very thin woman, with long grey hair, was crossing the street in front of the diner. She held Owen Gurlach by the arm and seemed to almost drag him against his will.

"Who is that woman with Owen?" Aspen asked.

"His mother," Warren said. "Helen Gurlach…she's mean as a snake. It hurts me to watch her drag her own kid around like that."

Aspen had a strong desire to speak to the woman. He also wanted to try and interact with Owen. However, right now, the top priority was finding Jacob. Warren and Aspen pulled into the driveway at Jacob Myers' house. It was a very nice ranch-style home, well-kept, and inviting. Jacob came to the door. His parents were still at work. Jacob took Aspen and Warren into the living room. Jacob was very handsome, and extremely well-groomed. His blonde hair was perfectly trimmed. He wore designer clothes and shoes. Aspen looked around the living room. The house was immaculate. Nothing was out of place. In fact, everything seemed to be perfect…too perfect.

Warren began.

"Jacob, we just want to talk to you about Emily. She mentioned you several times in her diary. She seemed to be uh…very concerned about you. She even said she was afraid you would do something really bad. Can you tell us why she might have thought that?"

"Well," Jacob answered. "She was a good friend, and I told her all my problems."

"Do you have lots of problems?" Warren asked.

Jacob looked extremely uneasy. He stared out the window for a moment.

"More than most people around here," he answered.

Aspen was already seeing many pictures in his mind. He saw images of Jacob standing on the street. Kids were taunting him. Then, one boy picked up a rock and threw it at Jacob.

"Jacob," Aspen said calmly. "I am autistic, and I have some psychic abilities. Do people pick on you for some reason? I'm getting some pretty strong images in my head."

Jacob sat silently for a moment. A tear came from his left eye. Then, he felt years of anger and frustration welling up inside.

"Kids pick on me a lot," he said. "I imagine that's why Emily was worried about me."

Aspen continued. Again, as he had with Jess, he spoke very calmly.

"Jacob. I've been picked on all my life. Many people have called me a retard, or even a lunatic. I've even been physically beaten up by some people, and Chief Dale most certainly understands what it's like to be picked on. So, feel free to tell us what you are thinking."

Jacob sat back on the couch as tears flowed down his face.

"You can't tell my parents," he said through sobs. "They're real…religious. They would KILL me if they knew."

Aspen spoke for Jacob.

"Are you gay, Jacob?"

Jacob gave out a huge sob. Rivers of tears poured from his eyes. He took a tissue from the box in front of him, and blew his nose.

"Yeah," he said. "The kids around here have figured it out. I have a boyfriend. They are ALWAYS picking on us! They even throw rocks at us!"

Warren spoke.

"So, that's why Emily was so worried about you in her diary?"

Jacob nodded between sobs. There was a long silence. Aspen and Warren could both relate to Jacob's pain.

"Jacob," Warren finally said. "I can find someone for you to talk to. I know someone who can help. As for those people picking on you…you need to let me know when that happens, so I can stop it."

"I'm not worried about them," Jacob replied. "It's my parents! They believe gay people are evil!! What the hell am I supposed to do about them?! Don't you know? The Bible says it's an abomination for two men to sleep together!"

"Jacob," Aspen said. "The Bible says many things that are wrong today. For example, it tells me that a man may kill his wife if she is unfaithful to him. The Old Testament is full of rules. However, the New Testament is the book of love. Christ taught us to love everyone…no exceptions. You will have to talk to your parents at some point about it, Jacob. Perhaps the Chief and I could be there with you…or maybe someone else who you trust very much. You cannot live your life in fear. You have every right to be who you are, just as I do, or the Chief does."

Warren gazed at Aspen in surprise. He was shocked at such a powerful, understanding response from one who seemed to be such a nerd.

"Well," Jacob said. "They'll be home soon. I'm not ready to talk to them today...but maybe soon. Could you please leave, so I can pull myself together? I really don't know what to tell you about Emily, except that I really miss her."

Warren patted Jacob on the shoulder.

"Remember what I told you," he said. "I can help."

Jacob nodded. Aspen and Warren headed home for dinner with Sherry.

Chapter 6 - Renfro Town Council

That evening at dinner, Sherry had prepared all of Aspen's favorites. Officer Mays had told her what he liked. She had shrimp with butter, and asparagus spears. She had toothpicks at each place so everyone could use them to pick up the shrimp, and Aspen wouldn't feel out of place. She also made sure everyone had a straw for drinks.

"This shrimp is delicious, Sherry," Aspen said.

Sherry smiled. She had become quite fond of Aspen in a short time. She and Warren had no children, and she liked doting on their guest. Warren, however, was not as comfortable with the toothpicks, but he made do. He knew it was polite, and he wanted to please Sherry.

"Well," Warren said, as he finished. "No time for dessert... town council meeting tonight."

"Aw," Sherry complained. "Can't you skip it... just this once. I made white cake with vanilla cream icing."

Aspen immediately perked up. That was his favorite cake.

"Afraid not, "Warren said. "I've got to go."

"Perhaps, I should also go," Aspen said. "We could possibly have cake when we return?"

"Oh," Sherry said, with a smile. "That sounds like a plan. I'll have it all ready for you boys when you get back."

"And a glass of milk?" Aspen ventured.

"You bet," Sherry said.

When Aspen and Warren walked into the fire hall, it was about half full. At the front table were the council members. Mayor, Ernie Newlen, sat in the middle, by the podium. Others at the table were, Dalton Keeler, Mavis Confer, Pete Corbit, Ed Glossner and Dwayne Zerby. Aspen sat in the front row, as Warren took his place at the front table next to Ernie.

"All right," Ernie said. "Let's get things goin' here."

Everyone in the room stood for the Pledge of Allegiance, and a short prayer, led by Father Marcinkevage.

"Thank you, Father," Ernie continued. "OK…The first order of business is the roll call. Let it be shown in the record that members present at tonight's meeting are myself, Chief Dale, and council members Keeler, Confer, Corbit, Glossner and Zerby."

Ernie paused and looked around the room, and sighed.

"Has anyone seen Red Markle?" Ernie asked.

Someone yelled from the back, "He's still up in Canada fishin."

"Okay," Ernie replied. "Let it be shown that Red Markle is STILL in Canada. Alright…on to the first item on the agenda. The game commission came in this week to talk about what we can do about the mange epidemic in bears. As you all know, mange is really killin' lots of bears. This is a serious problem, and the game commissioner I talked with said we've got to get folks to quit feedin' the bears. It really causes the mange to spread."

There was a buzz of conversation around the room. One person yelled out.

"Aw, Ernie! It don't hurt nothin' to feed the bears."

"Now that ain't true," Ernie said. "The mites that carry mange fall off and get onto other bears when they get in a big group to feed. If you put out corn, you're spreadin' mange! This is serious folks! This mange epidemic could wipe out the bear population."

"Well," Dwayne Zerby said, "I just put a little corn out for the squirrels. That don't hurt nothin'. My wife likes to watch the squirrels."

"Well now Dwayne," Ernie continued. "That's just what I'm talkin' about. Do you really think the bears come wanderin' in at night and tell each other not to eat that corn, because it's the squirrel corn?"

"Well," Dwayne said. "I don't put that much out."

Ernie could feel his blood pressure rising.

"Dammit Dwayne!" he shouted. "That's the problem! Everybody's been doin' this stuff for years, and now it's catchin' up with us! Do you really want to kill off all the bears in Pennsylvania?!"

"Well, I don't see what a little corn is gonna hurt," Dwayne persisted.

Ed Glossner spoke up.

"Maybe we ought to table this issue for next meeting."

Ernie sighed.

"Well, alright, but I'm bringing the game commission in to speak about this at our next council meeting."

Again, there was a buzz throughout the room. Aspen looked around. Everyone seemed to be enjoying the arguing that was taking place.

"Now, Ernie stated. "We've got the Fireman's Pig Roast this Saturday. We need to sort this out first. As usual, it'll be a buffet, and the cost is seven dollars for adults and three dollars for kids under…What is it, uh ten?"

"Twelve," Everyone yelled.

"Ok. My mistake…twelve. Now, thanks to Dale Farms for providin' the pig. This year, we were talkin' about closing two blocks of Main Street to make more room."

There was mumbling and discussion throughout the hall. One person called out.

"Why should we do that?"

"Well," Ernie continued. "Last year, we had so many people that the merchants downtown figured it might help their businesses to have main street closed off to parking, so they could set up tables with merchandise. Maybe people might want to do a little shoppin' after they eat, and we thought we might have some live music too."

The hall was silent. Ernie gave another deep sigh. He half expected to hear crickets chirping over the silence at any minute.

"We never done that before, Ernie," Dalton Keeler said.

"Yeah, Dalton. I know. It's a new idea. I'm tryin' to get people in the community to be a little more active and support the merchants downtown."

"But we always just had it in the parking lot at the fire hall," someone said. "That's just how we always done it!"

"What about the cleanup?" Ed Glossner commented. "It's gonna make an awful mess of Main Street."

"Well, hell," Mavis Confer practically shouted. "I think it's a good idea. Might get more people out of the house, and they might even have a good time!"

Mavis was a large woman. She ran the local feed store, and she had the habit of stomping her large, booted foot on the concrete floor when she made a point. This caused Aspen to jump, but everyone else seemed to be used to it.

"I don't know," Ed Glossner said again. "It's gonna' add an awful lot to cleanin' up afterwards."

"I'll bring a couple of small dumpsters down if that'll help," Pete Corbit said. Pete was the local garbage hauler. Ernie smiled.

"Well, there ya' go," he said. "That's the way. Thanks, Pete! Now, let's have a vote. All in favor of tryin' this, say yea."

All council members raised their hands and said yea, except for Ed.

"I'll abstain," Ed said.

Ernie shook his head.

"OK. Let the record show that the majority of town council agreed to close main street for the pig roast."

Ernie smiled a bit, as he glanced down at Warren.

"OK," Ernie said. "Our next item…Do we pay for blacktop on Edwin Street, or do we want to oil and chip."

"Oil and chip," Everyone yelled.

"That's how we always done it," Dwayne Zerby said.

"Yeah, oil and chip holds up better," Pete Confer interjected. "No need to do it different."

Ernie was hoping for blacktop, but he decided not to push it, since he had won the pig roast battle.

He asked for a vote.

"Ok…Anyone oppose the oil and chip job for Edwin Street?"

"I'll abstain," Ed Glossner said.

"Aw, Ed," Mavis Confer yelled. "Have a backbone fer' once. How the hell did you ever make a decision to git' married to Rose?!"

"SHE asked HIM!" Someone yelled from the back.

Everyone laughed. Aspen smiled. Ed grew red and lowered his bald head.

"Alright, Alright," Ernie shouted. "No need fer' that. We all know Ed just likes to be a little cautious…nothin' wrong with that. Now…on to the big item. Warren has been in touch with the county, and they're thinkin' of puttin' in a county prison up this way."

There was a buzz through the room. Ernie held up his hands.

"Now, quiet down please. This would bring some jobs up our way, and it would also help us out with some tax dollars. Only thing is," Ernie breathed a deep sigh before continuing. "they will only do it if we agree to some flood protection…a levee."

The room went wild. People immediately began arguing.

Ernie had to use his gavel for the first time.

"We can't afford no levee, Ernie!" Dalton Keeler exclaimed.

"This is gonna' ruin' fishin' in this area," Ed Glossner said.

"Now, listen!" Ernie yelled. "We don't have to pay for this. It would be built by the Army Corps of Engineers and paid for by the government!"

"Sure, and our taxes will go through the roof!" somebody yelled.

"We don't need no flood control!" somebody else hollered.

The crowd returned to a roar. Ernie tried and tried to quiet the hall, but to no avail. Finally, he looked at Warren. They were both disgusted. Ernie yelled over the crowd that they would table the matter, and he finally adjourned the meeting.

As promised, Sherry had cake and milk ready for Aspen and Warren when they got home. Aspen used two napkins, one in case he got any icing on his face, and the other for wiping the corners of his mouth after sipping milk.

"Warren," Aspen commented. "I'm noticing the people here seem to have some difficulty accepting any, um…different ideas."

"Yeah," Warren said, as he chuckled. "You might say that. That's why this town is dying Aspen. You heard how old Ernie had to fight tonight, just to get them to agree to close the street for the pig roast…and building a levee for flood control?! Forget it. It'll never happen."

"But flood control would help this town," Aspen responded.

"Sure it would," Shelly intervened. "Warren, eat your cake. Aspen, the folks around here want everything to stay just the way it is."

"Why?" Aspen said with confusion.

"Fear," Sherry continued. "The people here fear what is outside Renfro. They stay in their safe little town, and try to keep it from changing. Do you want more cake, Aspen?"

"Oh, no thank you. It was delicious, but I'm quite tired. I think I'll go to my room."

"Well," Sherry said, as she gave a little wink to Warren, "you make sure you get rested up for our get-together tomorrow night."

"Excuse me?" Aspen asked.

"We're having a nice big dinner tomorrow night, and I invited Katy to join us."

Warren looked stunned.

"Katy?" Aspen asked.

"Yes, Katy Rosamilia. Warren told me you two seemed to really hit it off at the diner, so I thought she could join us."

"Oh my," Aspen said, half gasping.

He glanced at Warren. Warren glanced at Sherry. Sherry smiled.

"It will be nice," Sherry said, as she cleared the cake plates.

Warren flashed a nervous grin at Aspen. He immediately regretted having told Sherry about Katy and Aspen hitting it off, but it was too late.

"Well," Aspen said. "I'll be off to bed. Goodnight."

"Goodnight!" Sherry and Warren said simultaneously.

Sherry walked to the kitchen. Warren was right on her heels.

"Baby," Warren exclaimed! "How could you DO that?!

"Oh, trust me," Sherry said. "It will be fine. We'll just have a nice dinner together. It will be good for Aspen. I KNOW it. It's my…feminine instinct."

Warren spoke softly.

"Sweet Jesus, help us."

"What was that?" Sherry called.

"Oh nothin' baby…nothin"

In the morning, Aspen went for his run. He now waited until the sun was up, since his encounter with the bear. As he ran past the old railroad buildings, he saw someone walking toward him. As he got closer, he realized it was Owen Gurlach.

"Owen," Aspen exclaimed! "What are you doing out here alone?"

Owen kept his distance. He was in tattered clothes. His jeans looked as if they had never been washed, and his t-shirt was ripped in several places.

Aspen stood patiently, without saying anything. He thought maybe Owen wanted to show him something, but it seemed that Owen was simply sizing Aspen up. After a few minutes, an old pickup truck appeared.

"Owen!" Helen Gurlach yelled. "Get over here! I been lookin' all over for ya'!"

Owen turned and walked to the truck. Helen hit the gas and sped off.

Although Owen had not been able to speak a word, Aspen felt great energy in his presence. Owen was indeed very intelligent. Aspen felt he needed to spend some more time with him.

Chapter 7 - Dinner With Katy

That evening, Aspen was a little nervous about dinner with Katy, but he was looking forward to seeing her. He calmed himself by remembering what his mother told him when he was a boy and felt anxious.

"Always smile and be yourself, Aspen. If people can't love you the way you are, they aren't worth being around."

He finished laying out the clothes he would wear to dinner. He was glad he had brought a white dress shirt, and bow tie. It was a clip-on, but he liked it. He also had khaki pants, and he had scrubbed his white sneakers with some bleach that Sherry had given him. They were pure white. Sherry had even run them in the dryer for him. He had also asked her for some hair gel. After he finished dressing, he looked at himself in the large, oval mirror in his room.

He smiled.

"Hello Katy," he practiced. "You look very nice this evening. Please allow me to take your jacket."

Yes, he felt good about this. He took one last look at himself and went downstairs.

"Oh, Aspen. Look at you!" Sherry exclaimed. "You look fantastic!"

Sherry walked over and straightened his collar.

Warren walked in and smiled.

"Woah!" Warren said. "Don't you look fine!"

Warren's brother, Thomas, and his girlfriend, Nancy, were also coming to dinner. The doorbell rang. It was Katy. Aspen sat up very straight on the couch. Then, he remembered it was polite to stand when a lady came in the room, so he sprang up like a rabbit coming out of a hole. He grinned, and stiffly walked over to Katy.

"Hi Aspen!" Katy said, with a big smile.

Aspen was suddenly at a loss for words. He couldn't remember any of the greetings he had practiced. He smiled the biggest smile he could muster, and gave out a small chuckle. He felt himself turning red in the face. Finally, he managed to speak.

"Hello! I cleaned my sneakers very well for tonight."

Katy giggled.

"Oh, Aspen! They look great!"

Her comment relaxed Aspen. His courage welled up inside.

"May I take your jacket?"

"Oh, thank you," Katy said.

The front door opened, and Thomas and Nancy came in. Everyone greeted one another and chatted, as Sherry busily made preparations. Aspen and Katy sat on the couch. Aspen completely relaxed as Katy told him about her day at the diner. Aspen then told her about his encounter in town with the bear, and they both laughed.

Sherry had prepared the same chicken breast dinner that Aspen had enjoyed on his first day in Renfro. Nobody minded that all the chicken was cut in neat, bite-sized squares, and everyone drank with a straw. For dessert, Sherry served white cake, with vanilla cream icing once again. Everyone got a glass of milk to accompany it, and two napkins.

After dinner, Thomas entertained everyone with stories of his childhood days with Warren. Thomas was a wonderful storyteller and kept everyone laughing. His girlfriend, Nancy, was very pretty. She was white, and Aspen couldn't help but wonder if that caused problems for them in Renfro, with so many bigoted people. They seemed to be very close. Thomas held Nancy's hand for most of the night. While he was listening to Thomas tell a story about tractor racing with Warren, Aspen felt Katy gently take his hand. At first, he tensed up a bit, but her touch was so gentle, the stress gradually slipped from his body. He looked over at her, and she smiled at him with great kindness, and understanding. He had not felt such tenderness since he had been with his mother.

As the evening ended, Aspen got up to fetch Katy's jacket. Thomas and Nancy left first. As Aspen and Katy walked to the door, Warren and Sherry stayed in the other room to give them privacy.

Aspen," Katy said. "I know it's hard for you, but may I give you a hug?"

Again, Aspen felt the tension return. He had never hugged anyone except his parents. For years, he had done nothing but knuckle bumps. He closed his eyes, and although his body was completely rigid, he threw his arms around Katy. Sherry's curiosity got the best of her, and she peeked around the door frame into the room. Warren quickly pulled her back.

"Warren!" she whispered. "I just want to see how it's going?"

Warren spoke softly but sternly.

"Woman! You keep out of this."

Katy warmly returned Aspen's embrace. She felt him relax after a few seconds. She gently took his hand again.

"Maybe you could stop by the diner tomorrow and visit."

"Oh," Aspen returned. "I'd like that very much!"

Katy had seen Sherry sneak a peek. She smiled.

"Goodnight Sherry!"

"Goodnight Katy!" Sherry's voice seemed to come out of nowhere, since Warren was still holding on to her.

"Bye Warren!"

"Bye Katy! Thanks for coming!" Warren called.

That night, Warren and Sherry were relaxing in bed, and talking about the evening.

"You really like are attached to old Aspen, aren't you?" Warren said.

Sherry nodded.

"I really am. He's so innocent…like the little boy we never got to have. I think you like having him around too."

"Yeah," Warren said. "He's really grown on me."

"You know what I think?" Sherry stated. "I think maybe Aspen acts the way people ought to, and the rest of us are kind of screwed up."

How do you mean?" Warren asked.

"Well, he's very direct. He doesn't beat around the bush. He's honest, and he has a very innocent, kind heart.

He doesn't need a lot to be happy. He takes everyone as they are. So what if he has some quirks? Who knows? Maybe he'll really be able to find out what happened to Emily."

Chapter 8 - Lucien

Lucien Gurlach was driving on an old logging road with his brother, Owen. Owen was flapping his hands. He was nervous because Lucien was driving very fast, and the old dirt road was full of ruts and potholes.

"What's wrong, Owen?" Lucien asked, with a laugh. "Too rough for ya'"

The old Ford pickup was barely staying on the road in some places, yet Lucien continued to hit the gas. As he came to a long, straight stretch in the road, Lucien spotted a groundhog. He smiled.

"Look, buddy," Lucien bellowed. "It's an easy ten points!"

Lucien aimed the truck. The truck made a small jump as it ran over the unsuspecting creature. Lucien laughed.

"Ha! We got him, little brother!"

Owen sat back in his seat. His eyes were full of tears.

"Aw, don't worry Owen," Lucien bellowed. "Plenty of groundhogs out there!"

The truck pulled into an old house along the road. It was a dilapidated old two-story, wood-frame house. Weeds grew up all around it. It had been empty for years.

"You stay here, little brother," Lucien commanded. "I'll be right back after I take care of some business."

The house was quiet. Lucien climbed the broken stairs to the back door. He pulled a pistol out of his jacket and kicked in the back door. Still, there was no sound. Lucien disappeared into the house, as Owen sat motionless in the truck, still crying about the groundhog.

After a few minutes, Owen heard Lucien yelling at someone.

"You holdin' out on me?!" Lucien screamed. "You're supposed to be selling, and you're using all the junk I'm givin' you! You owe me big time, now pay up, you son of a bitch!"

A terrified voice answered.

"Next week, Lucien! I promise! Oh God No! PLEASE!"

There was a single gunshot. After a pause, Lucien came out, dragging a man's body. He opened a door in the ground. It was an old well. He dragged the lifeless body over to the well, and dropped it in. Owen waited for a splash, but the well was dry, so he heard only an empty thud as the body hit bottom.

Lucien returned to the truck. Owen was rocking, back and forth nervously, in the passenger seat, flapping his hands. Lucien smiled, as if he was admiring the scenery around the old house.

"Relax, little brother," Lucien said. "There, that's taken care of. I'm starving. You wanna' get somethin' to eat?"

Chapter 9 – Jacob

Again, Warren and Aspen returned to Emily's diary. Warren carefully went through entries looking for clues. Aspen held the diary in his hands, hoping for some information that would pop into his head. There was nothing, except for the vision of Abe's birthday party. Both men were feeling frustration and despair.

"Warren," Aspen asked. "Have many people gone missing from Renfro?"

"I'm afraid so," Warren answered. "These woods go from here pretty much up to the New York state line. There are lots of people up to no good, and there's a lot of ground for us cops to cover when somebody does something wrong. Warren's phone rang. He looked at Aspen, then got up and left the room. Aspen could hear him talking. Warren sounded upset.

"OK. I'll be right there," Warren said before he hung up.

"Aspen," Warren said softly. "That was the coroner's office. I have to go back to Jacob's house."

"Did something bad happen?" Aspen asked.

"Yes. Jacob told his parents he was gay. It didn't go well. His dad got pretty mad and told Jacob he would have to get out of the house for good. Jacob went to his room, and well…he hung himself."

Aspen sat silently. He was devastated. Perhaps, he had caused this.

"Now Aspen," Warren continued. "I know what you're thinking. Just because you tried to encourage Jacob to be himself doesn't mean you are to blame. Jacob's dad is…well…he's pretty strict, to say the least. He's the one who made Jacob take his life. He never should have thrown his own son out of the house like that."

Aspen sat silently. Finally, he spoke.

"Should I go with you?"

"No…I think it's best if I go alone."

Aspen sat, looking as if he might cry.

"I think I'll go home and see Sherry. I'm missing my mom right now. Sherry reminds me of her."

"OK," Warren answered. "That's a good idea. Take the rest of the day off. I'll see you at dinner time."

Aspen went home. Sherry had heard the news. She had cake and a glass of milk ready for him. Aspen ate the cake and drank the milk. However, he remained in his room that night, and did not come down for supper.

After going through Emily's diary again the next morning, Aspen went to the diner to visit Katy, as he had promised. She smiled as Aspen walked in. She finished waiting on tables. Aspen waited patiently by the door. Finally, she got away from her customers and gave Aspen a warm hug.

"How are you?" she asked.

"I am sad," Aspen said, with his head down.

"I have a few minutes," Katy said. "Let's sit down. I heard about Jacob."

They went to a table and chatted, Katy on one side of the booth and Aspen on the other.

"It wasn't your fault, Aspen. I know it's sad, but don't blame yourself."

"I was trying to encourage him to be brave, but it was not my place," Aspen replied.

"Aspen," Katy continued. "You, of all people, know that you can't live your life in fear. That's what Jacob was doing. You did the right thing, but sometimes bad things happen anyway…even when somebody does the right thing."

Aspen nodded.

"Katy," he said. "Why are people here so fearful of anything different?"

Katy thought for a moment.

"Things haven't changed much around here in over a hundred years, Aspen. When people live in isolation for a long time, it does things to them. People here are really afraid of the outside world."

Katy let Aspen sit quietly for a minute. She had to get back to work, so she decided to change the subject to their dinner date.

"I had a great time last night," Katy said.

"It was very nice," Aspen responded. "I like the way Sherry makes her chicken."

"Me too! She is very fond of you Aspen."

"She reminds me of my mother...not just her cooking skills, but her mannerisms."

Sherry reached over and touched Aspens hand.

"Oh my!" Aspen said. "That is a very nice bracelet!"

"Thanks! It's carved out of wood," Katy said. "Owen made it for me. He comes in here sometimes. I think he's lonely."

"Owen? May I see it?" Aspen asked.

Katy slipped off the bracelet and laid it in Aspen's hand. Aspen gazed with great admiration at the beads. The workmanship was incredible. Each wooden bead was hand carved, with a tiny face, and each bead had been carefully hollowed out to fit on a string. Suddenly, Aspen sat up very straight. His eyes stared at Katy, but he didn't seem to see her. Katy looked concerned.

"Katy!" Aspen said without emotion. "This bracelet! You said Owen made it?!"

"Yes." Katy was looking worried. She thought she had done something wrong.

Aspen saw images…strong images. He saw Emily. She was in a crude cell of some kind. She was dressed in a nightgown. Her hair was dirty, and it hung down over her face. She was barefoot. Aspen also saw images of a shack in the woods. The images suddenly stopped.

"Katy!" he spoke normally again. "Owen must know where Emily is! I'm sorry. I must go find Warren! We have to find Owen! May I please keep this bracelet for a little while?"

"What?! Really?! Of course. Keep it as long as you need to."

Aspen got up, still somewhat dazed. He managed to give Katy a hug and went out the door of the diner. He knew now that Owen held the key to finding Emily.

Aspen rushed down the street to the police station. Warren was not there. Two Pennsylvania state troopers who were friends of Warren, were there eating lunch.

"Pardon me, officers," Aspen said. "Have you seen the Chief?"

"Nope," one trooper said. "We're just passing through. We thought we'd have lunch with Warren, but he must be eating lunch somewhere else today…maybe with the wife."

"Thank you," Aspen said, as he ran out the door.

Warren, had, in fact, started to head home for lunch when he spotted Lucien Gurlach's old truck at the town bar. He decided to make a bold move. As luck would have it, Aspen ran by the bar, and saw the police car parked in front. He caught Warren going in the door.

"Warren!" he said. "It's Owen! Owen can take us to Emily! I know it!"

"How do you know?" Warren asked.

"This bracelet. It's Katy's. I'm getting much information from it! We need to find Owen right now!"

"Ok," Warren said. "But first, I need to take care of something here, and you just helped me. You wait until I signal you. Then, you come over and sit by me. We're going to have a little talk with Lucien. He isn't in town very much, so I don't want to miss this chance."

Lucien sat at a booth drinking a beer and smoking a cigar. Warren slowly walked over to him and sat down across from him. Lucien gave him a smart-ass smile.

"Well," he said calmly. "It's Renfro's motha-fuckah' cop, come to pay me a visit."

Warren looked back at Lucien with complete calm.

"I know you were involved in Emily's disappearance Lucien. I don't know just how, but I know you were messed up in it, and I'm going to find out everything."

Lucien paused, and gave a chuckle.

"Oh shit, Dale," he laughed. "You been tryin' to get me for fourteen years."

Lucien held out his hands.

"OK, Chief," he said. "Slap those cuffs on me!"

Warren ignored him. Lucien finally lowered his hands.

Warren sat silently for a moment. He wanted to choose his words carefully.

"Well, Lucien...this time I got something you couldn't plan on."

Lucien smiled coldly. He inhaled smoke from his cigar, and blew it toward Warren. Then, he faked a serious look.

"Ooh," he said in a mockingly serious tone. "Now what's that? You got me shakin' in my white-ass, redneck boots over here."

Warren turned and motioned to Aspen.

Aspen walked over and sat by Warren. He was still out of breath from running.

"Hello, Mr. Gurlach," Aspen said.

"This is Aspen," Warren said. "He's helping us with Emily's case. Aspen has, some psychic abilities."

Lucien burst into laughter. After a long laugh, he looked into Warren's eyes.

"Is that a fact? A psychic! Haw! You reached the point where you had to go and get yourself a...voodoo man? Ooh! That's how fuckin' desperate you are, Chief?"

"Aspen can talk to Owen," Warren interrupted.

Aspen glanced at Warren. He wasn't quite sure he could actually "talk: to Owen, but he didn't want to disagree with Warren.

"Owen!" Lucien laughed again. "My simple-minded brother, Owen! Oh, Lord almighty help me! Well, Chief Warren...and voodoo man...you bring it on. My little brother can't get dressed without lots a' help! So, if you think he can help you find little Emily...you go for it!"

Lucien got up to leave. Aspen surprised him by suddenly grabbing his arm. He concentrated to see if he would get any information from holding Lucien. He got visions by the second...shootings, drug deals, and a strong vision of a big man...tall, with red hair and a full beard. He clutched Lucien's forearm, until Lucien finally pulled away angrily. Aspen looked Lucien square in the eyes.

"Mr. Gurlach," Aspen said coldly. "I believe there is a special corner of Hell reserved for people like you...people who discriminate against others and cause great pain. It's very hot there, and most painful."

For the first time, Lucien looked slightly uneasy. He straightened his jacket, then gave a disgusted chuckle as he walked out of the bar.

Chapter 10 - Owen

Warren sped through Renfro to the Gurlach house. He asked Aspen about what he had seen when he held Lucien's arm.

"I saw so many terrible things, but the one thing that I kept seeing over and over was an image of a tall man…a big man, with red hair, and a big red beard."

"That's Red Markel!" Warren exclaimed. "He's a town councilman. He's supposed to be in Can…"

Warren paused. Shock came over his face.

"Oh my God! Why the hell didn't I think of it?!

"What is it?"! Aspen asked.

Warren spoke softly.

"Emily disappeared the day Red left for Canada to go fishing. Red's messed up in this, and he's messed up with Lucien, I bet!"

The squad car raced down the river road. Warren turned onto Eagleville Valley Road, an old road from the lumbering days. It was a narrow dirt road, with two deep ruts from tires, only wide enough for one car. Warren barely slowed down at all, and Aspen was bouncing, as if he were on a trampoline. In the distance, Aspen spotted an ancient log house. That was where the Gurlach family lived. Warren pulled in. He saw that Lucien's truck was not there.

"Let's see if Owen's here," Warren said.

They didn't have to wait long. Owen walked out the front door, as they approached the house. He seemed to expect them. He went right over to Aspen. Warren knocked on the door. Nobody answered. He cautiously entered the old home. With gun drawn, he silently surveyed the entire, filthy house. The stench was unbearable. Warren hated to think of poor Owen living this way. The home was a fire hazard, with a path through the trash. The water had been turned off long ago for non-payment, and rotting food covered the kitchen table. After checking each room, Warren went back outside.

"Nobody in there," he said.

Aspen had been "communicating" with Owen. He gently held Owen's forearm. Owen understood perfectly what Aspen was doing.

"They are on their way to Red's cabin," Aspen said. "Apparently, we upset Mr. Gurlach at the bar. Owen says Lucien called his mother to warn her. It seems Mrs. Gurlach is also involved."

"We're gonna' need some help." Warren said.

"There were two state troopers back at your office eating lunch. I stopped in there looking for you," Aspen exclaimed. "Perhaps they could be of help."

"Probably, but we need to get there now! Emily is probably at Red's cabin, and it's over this mountain!" Warren said.

Owen grabbed Aspen by the arm. Aspen looked down and saw Owen held some keys. Owen pulled Aspen toward an old Chevy pickup behind the log house.

"I will drive with Owen in that truck, Warren," Aspen said. "You must go get those other officers and meet us at Red's cabin."

"You?!" Warren practically yelled. "Aspen! Can you actually drive?!"

"I have never driven, but I have watched carefully as others did. It will be probably fine."

Before Warren could speak, Aspen and Owen ran to the old truck. Aspen was happy to see it was an automatic transmission. He started the engine with a huge roar, shifted into drive, and took off up the Eagleville Valley Road."

Warren stared in disbelief. He had no choice, but to go with Aspen's plan. He ran to the squad car and radioed the station.

"Come on! Come on, guys!" he said. "Please still be there!"

Finally, one of the troopers answered the radio, as Warren sped away from the Gurlach house. Warren told the cops to stay put. He would lead the troopers to Red's cabin.

"Sweet Jesus," Warren said. "Please don't let me fuck this up!"

Chapter 11 - A Country Drive

The old Chevy pickup bounced over the rocks and potholes with Aspen clutching the wheel. He alternated between hitting the accelerator, and the brake.

"Oh!! Aspen cried with every bump. "OH MY!"

He looked over at Owen, who was actually smiling, and enjoying the ride immensely. He looked as if he were on an amusement park ride. He even occasionally raised his arms in the air in complete joy. Aspen approached a long steep dip in the road.

"Hold on, Owen!"

The truck raced downhill and shot up the other side. Owen began to frantically point to the right. Aspen knew Owen wanted him to pull over. There was a small clearing, so Aspen steered for it, but he was slow to hit the brake. The truck slammed into a log and came to rest. Owen jumped out, and immediately started for the top of the hill. He stopped and looked back at Aspen. He signaled for Aspen to follow him, and they both began climbing to the top of the hill.

Owen was in amazing shape. Aspen thought, as he huffed and puffed, that Owen could run one of those insane marathon races up the side of mountains, and over boulder fields. Then, he saw Owen stop behind a huge oak tree. Aspen finally caught up. Owen was staring at the back of Red's cabin. It seemed that they had managed to arrive before Red and Helen. Owen silently led Aspen to the back door. He pulled a key from his pocket, and quietly opened the door.

Aspen walked with Owen into the dark shack. There was a small kitchen area. In the middle of the room was an old bed. Owen pulled a cord dangling from a single light bulb. The tiny bulb barely provided any useful light. Aspen heard a small cry from the side of the room. He gazed in that direction, and what he saw sent him into shock. There was an actual handmade jail cell. It contained a small bed, and a bucket for a toilet. Huddled in the back was a young girl. Aspen peeked in cautiously.

"Emily?" he said carefully.

There was no answer, but the young girl crouched down in fear.

"Emily," Aspen repeated. "We're here to help you."

Owen touched Aspen's arm. Aspen jumped in fright.

"Aah! What is it Owen?"

Owen handed Aspen the key to the cell.

"Oh," Aspen said. "Very good Owen! Very good!"

Aspen gently turned the key in the old lock and opened the door. Emily was dressed just as she had been in Aspen's vision. She wore an old, tattered, short nightgown. She was dirty, and half-frozen. She was crouched in the corner of the cell…shivering, and terrified. She finally looked up at Aspen, as he crept closer.

"Emily," he said. "I'm Aspen. I'm not here to harm you. In fact, Owen and I want to help you get out of this place. I want to take you home to your mother."

Emily looked over at Owen. She knew Owen was kind. She trusted him. If he had brought Aspen, she decided, it must be safe. She paused, then cautiously reached out a hand. Aspen gently took her hand and led her out of the cell.

"Very good, Emily," Aspen said soothingly.

They all stopped in horror. There was the sound of footsteps outside! The back door crashed open! It was Red Markle, and Helen Gurlach was with him.

"Quickly!" Aspen cried. "Out the front door!"

Aspen pushed Owen ahead of him and held Emily by the hand. Owen made it out the door, but Emily was caught by Red.

"No!" Red yelled. "Stay with me, Emily! You'll come to love me! I promise!"

Emily screamed, as Red held her around her waist. Aspen picked up a piece of wood by the fireplace, and smacked it down on Red's back, knocking the wind out of him. It was just enough to loosen Red's grip on Emily, and Aspen pulled her toward the front door. Red pulled out a gun, from his jacket pocket, and charged after Emily, with Helen right on his heels. Just as they got outside, there was a shout from the bottom of the hill.

"Drop it, Red!"

It was Warren. He had the two state troopers with him. All three officers had their rifles drawn, and fixed on Red. He looked at the police officers and knew there was no escape. Finally, he dropped his gun. As the officers began to climb the hill, a rifle shot rang out, and Red dropped to the ground. He was dead…a single shot to the head. Lucien was at the top of the hill with a deer rifle. He shot again, hitting a state trooper in the shoulder. Helen looked down at Red and dropped to her knees, sobbing. As pathetic as their relationship had been, Red was the only man who had ever paid attention to her.

She took Red's gun, held it in her mouth and pulled the trigger. Her body dropped on top of Red's.

Aspen continued to lay on the ground. He and Owen were both covering Emily's body to protect her. Lucien and Warren continued to fire at each other, but Lucien had the advantage of being at the top of the hill. To everyone's surprise, Owen reached out and grabbed the gun from Helen's dead hand. He turned and fired at his older brother. Years of anger and frustration came erupted. Owen yelled, and charged right at Lucien, firing several rounds.

Lucien was shocked. He couldn't believe Owen was capable of this. As his concentration wavered, Lucien's finger tightened, and he fired one last shot, hitting Owen in the leg. Owen fell to the ground, writhing in pain.

"Oh, God!" Lucien said. "No! Owen!" he yelled. "I… I didn't mean to!"

Warren and the uninjured trooper started up the hill after Lucien. Lucien turned, and retreated to his old truck. He tore off down the old logging road. Meanwhile, the injured state trooper radioed for help. Warren and the other trooper ran to Aspen, Emily, and Owen.

"Emily," Aspen asked. "Were you shot?"

Emily shook her head.

Warren took off his belt and began to make a tourniquet for Owen.

"You're gonna' be ok, Owen," Warren said. "You just sit tight. Help is on the way."

Aspen looked down at Owen and Emily. It dawned on him that they needed to be nurtured, just as his mother had nurtured him when he was a boy. He ran to the cabin and found two old blankets. He took them outside and carefully wrapped Owen and Emily in them. Aspen felt so good inside, as he wrapped them. It felt good to nurture. Even though Owen was in pain, he smiled up at Aspen. Emily did as well. Aspen realized that perhaps all of Renfro needed nurturing. Maybe that was why the town was dying…from a lack of nurturing. The people there felt alone and frightened, so all they knew how to do was feel hatred and anger…like Lucien.

Owen, Emily, and the injured trooper were taken to the medical center. Owen and the trooper were fortunate to have received only relatively minor injuries. Emily was physically in fair shape, but mentally, she was in for a long journey to recovery. Aspen was exhausted and returned to Dale Farm for some quiet time.

Chapter 12 - Goodbye Renfro

Over the next two days, Warren worked with the state police to piece together what had happened. As it turned out, Red Markel had been sexually abusing teenage girls, from Pennsylvania to Canada, for years. He also had a strange partnership with Helen Gurlach. Helen loved Red. She loved him so much, she allowed him to pull her into his perverse world. She fed the girls, and kept them alive, until Red tired of them. Lucien had assisted in helping to kidnap Emily, because Red had become an active partner in the Gurlach heroin business. Lucien was protecting his investment.

Later that morning, Aspen and Katy walked in to see Warren, and the other officers. Warren filled them in on what they had unraveled so far.

"Warren…What about Lucien?" Aspen asked. "He's still out there?"

"Well," Warren answered. "He shot a state trooper, so this is a federal crime now. Over the next couple of days, Renfro will be seeing a lot of FBI, state troopers, and probably U. S. Marshals. We'll find him…probably take a while. Lucien knows every inch of those woods."

"How is Emily?" Katy asked.

"Physically, not too bad." Warren said. "Mentally, we'll have to see. She's home with her mom, and that'll help. She's getting counseling. Time will tell."

Aspen thought for a moment. Something else was really bothering him.

"And Owen?"

"That's the best news, Aspen. You've had quite an impact on me and Sherry. We're going to see about taking Owen in with us."

Aspen smiled.

"Oh, I like that idea very much. That will be very good for Owen…and for you and Sherry!"

"Well, enough about us," Warren said. "What about you two? You really hit it off."

Katy gently took Aspen's arm. She was beaming.

"I'm driving down to Williamstown this weekend to visit Aspen."

"Yes," Aspen said. "I'm taking Katy to all of my favorite places…the library, the park, and the movies…."

"And," Katy interrupted. "Aspen will be coming to visit me in Renfro too."

"Yes," Aspen said. "Perhaps I will get a driver's license!"

Warren smiled.

"God help us," he said as he laughed.

Back at Dale Farm, Aspen was taking one last walk around. Officer Mays was in the house, catching up on all the news with Warren and Sherry. Aspen looked down the river toward Renfro. Yes, it was a troubled little town, but he had hope for it. He started back toward the house. The chickens were in front of the barn. Aspen put his hood up and danced around them. The country life had not cured him of his fear of birds.

Mays came out the back door with Aspen's huge bag. He dragged it to the squad car and put it in the back. Warren, Sherry, and Katy followed him.

"Well, Aspen," he said. "You ready to go?"

"Yes, but I must say my goodbyes."

Aspen walked to Sherry. She had tears in her eyes.

"Thank you for everything, Sherry," Aspen said, barely able to hold tears back himself. "I will miss you, but I will be back."

Sherry hugged him tightly. Aspen didn't mind. In fact, he felt completely at ease.

"We're always here for you, Aspen."

Warren walked over and offered his knuckles for a bump. To his surprise, Aspen gave him a warm embrace. Now, Warren felt warm tears forming in his eyes.

"Couldn't have done it without you, buddy. Thanks for all your help. You brought Emily home."

Katy hugged Aspen and gave him a kiss on the cheek.

"I'll be down to see you Saturday."

Aspen smiled.

"That will be wonderful. I will make sure my sneakers are extra clean!"

Aspen and Mays turned and got into the car. They waved to everyone and headed down the river road.

"So," Mays said. "What's up with this Katy girl?"

"She is my girlfriend," Aspen replied.

"You got yourself a girlfriend?" Mays asked?

"Yes," Aspen replied. "Isn't she a...hottie?"

Mays laughed.

"Aspen," he said. "You old dawg!"

That week, at the Renfro town council meeting, a vote was taken on flood control. Surprisingly, it passed, and it was timid, old Ed Glossner who cast the deciding vote.

The End

Made in the USA
Middletown, DE
24 October 2020

22330167R00080